Disney's
The Fox and the Hound
Hide-and-Seek

 A GOLDEN BOOK · NEW YORK

randomhousekids.com
ISBN 978-0-375-83662-6 (trade) — ISBN 978-0-385-38972-3 (ebook)
Printed in the United States of America
20 19 18 17 16 15 14 13 12

Tod was a lively young fox who lived
on a farm. His friend Copper was a
long-eared, big-footed hound pup who
lived down the road. Tod and Copper
did everything together.

They swam
in the pond.

They chased chickens
out of the barn.

They helped Boomer the woodpecker and Dinky the sparrow hunt for caterpillars. Sometimes they just sat under the oak tree and talked with Big Mama the owl.

Every day as Tod watched Copper go
home, he felt a sad, empty feeling inside.
"Honey," said Big Mama, "that empty
feeling is called being lonely."

One afternoon when Copper came to play,
Tod was tired of chasing chickens and looking
for caterpillars and staying around the farm.

"Let's go exploring in the forest!" he said eagerly.

"That sounds like fun," Copper said. "I'll race
you across the meadow."

"You two ought to wait till tomorrow morning," Big Mama called after them. "It gets dark fast in the forest, and you might get lost."

"Don't worry," Tod said. "We'll be careful."

And off they ran.

It was cool and dim in the forest. The trees were close together and their leafy branches shut out the sky. The only sounds were the chirping of birds and the rustling of small animals in the underbrush.

"What a good place for hide-and-seek!" cried Tod. "Want to play, Copper? I'll hide, and you look for me."

"Okay," said Copper.
"I'll find you, too."
Copper covered his eyes
and started counting while
Tod looked for a place to hide.

"If I stay close by, he's sure to find me," Tod thought. So he ran past trees and mossy rocks and swam across a little stream. Then he ran some more. Finally, he stopped at a hollow tree stump.

"This is the perfect place," he thought. "Copper will never find me here!"

He crawled into the stump and curled up.
It was cozy and warm, and Tod was tired from
all the running he'd done. Before he knew it,
he was fast asleep.

Meanwhile, Copper had finished counting and was looking for Tod. He put his nose to the ground, as hound dogs do, and sniffed for Tod's scent.

He sniffed at a clump of tall grass. There was a beating of wings, and a quail flew out.

He sniffed at some
dry leaves under a big
beech tree. Two squirrels
jumped out and ran up
the tree.

He sniffed around a fallen log, and a prickly porcupine rattled its quills at him.

At last, Copper picked up Tod's scent. He followed it to the stream, and he swam across. But when he got to the other side and started sniffing again, there was no trace of Tod.

Copper began to get worried. "What if it gets dark before I find Tod?" he thought.

It *was* dark when Tod woke up.

"Copper didn't find me," he thought as he
climbed out of the tree stump. "Maybe he went
home without me. I'll never be able to find my
way home by myself."

Tod was frightened.

Suddenly, he heard something move behind him. He turned around. Two eyes gleamed in the darkness. "It must be a bear," Tod thought, trembling. "Oh, I wish Copper were here!" He was so scared that he began to cry.

"Tod, is that you?" a shaky little voice asked.
"Copper!" Tod exclaimed. "You found me!
I thought you were a bear."

"I'm so glad I found you," Copper said. "I was frightened all by myself in the dark."

"So was I," Tod said. "I thought you had gone home and left me here alone."

"I wouldn't do that," said Copper. "We're friends. Friends stick together and help each other out."

Tod and Copper huddled close to each other to keep warm. "It's not so scary in the forest when you have a friend to keep you company," Tod said.

"Everything's easier when you have a friend," said Copper. "Tomorrow morning, we'll help each other find the way home."

"No need to wait that long," said a voice above them.

It was Big Mama.

"I had a feeling you two might need some help," she said. "When you weren't back by sundown, I figured I'd better come looking for you."

"We're glad you did, Big Mama," Copper said. "Thank you."

"Well, honey, you're my friends," said Big Mama. "Friends take care of each other. Now, you just follow me and I'll have you home in no time."

When they were out of the forest and
across the meadow, Tod and Copper
started to say good-bye.

"Copper, will we always be friends?"
Tod asked.

"Forever and ever," said Copper.
"Maybe even longer than that."

The little hound started down the road to his home. This time, Tod didn't feel a bit lonely as he watched Copper go. He knew that no matter how often Copper left, he'd always come back. After all, he was a friend, and that's what friends do.